Postman Pat® and the Jumble Sale

SIMON AND SCHUSTER

It was Recycling Week in Greendale, and everyone was getting ready for the Jumble Sale.

"I must do my baking for the food stall!" said Sara. "But where can I put these geraniums Dorothy gave me?"

"Lucy's dad's got them in window boxes," said Julian.

"Good idea! Can you make me some, Pat?"

"Er, maybe later!" mumbled Pat.

"Have you finished with your newspaper, Dad?" asked Julian.

"No!" Pat whisked his paper away.

"Oh, Dad!" pleaded Julian. "It's Recycling Week. I need it!"

At the Post Office, Mrs Goggins had several large packages for Pat.

"These are all for the station," she told him. "And this . . . is for the school – be careful with it!"

"Oh! It's the little apple tree the children sent off for," smiled Pat.

Pat delivered the parcels to Nisha.

She gave Jess a saucer of milk. "Miaow!"

"Would you do me a favour, Pat?" Nisha asked. "A few people in the village have got things for the Jumble Sale. Could you pick them up on your post round?"

"No problem, Nisha. Just give me the list!"

"You can have these for the Jumble Sale too, Nisha!" said Ajay, staggering along the platform with some old toolboxes. "I'm fed up with tripping over them!"

At the school, the children were busy in the garden.

"Hi Dad!" called Julian. "Look at the flowers we planted."

"That's grand!" admired Pat. "And I have something here to make your garden even lovelier!"

"The apple tree! Thanks, Pat," said Jeff Pringle.

Julian and Meera had already dug a hole. They planted the tree, and Bill gave it a good watering.

"Let's hope it grows lots of apples!" said Tom.

Pat collected Jeff's jumble for Nisha.

"It's a cuckoo clock," said Jeff, "but it doesn't tell the time any more."

"And the cuckoo is all wonky," added Charlie.

Suddenly the cuckoo popped out:

"Cuck-oooo!"

Jess was startled.

"Miaow!"

"Don't worry, Jess," Pat laughed. "It's not a real bird!"

At the Thompson's farm, Dorothy was having trouble with birds too! The crows were eating all her lettuces.

"Shoo, you greedy crows. Get off!"

"Oh dear, Dorothy, the crows have certainly taken a fancy to your lettuces!" chuckled Pat.

"Not to worry, this scarecrow will keep them away," said Alf confidently. But when he stuck it into the ground, the rickety scarecrow fell to pieces!

Dorothy had an old sewing machine for Nisha.
Pat shoved it into the back of his van.

"Righto! Good luck with the crows, Dorothy."

"Thanks, Pat, I'll need it!"

At the church, there was a dreadful screeching noise.

It was the vicar!

"I used to play the violin when I was a boy," he said sadly. "It's been in the attic for years. I thought Nisha should have it for the jumble."

"Are you sure?" asked Pat.

"What the Lord giveth, the Lord also taketh away," sighed the vicar.

Pat's last stop was Dr Gilbertson's.

"You're just in time for coffee," she said.

But as Pat was about to sit down, the garden table collapsed!

"Oh dear. This old table was filled with woodworm,"
Dr Gilbertson explained. "What a shame, I do so like
sitting outside."

Pat dropped Nisha's jumble at the station.

"Oh my goodness, what wonderful things," she said.

"It'll be a grand Recycling Jumble," agreed Pat. "Mind you, I'm not so sure Reverend Timms wanted to give his violin away!"

Back home, Julian was pasting soggy slips of paper onto blown-up balloons.

"Have you seen the newspaper?" Pat asked him.

"Er, sorry, Dad . . . I needed it for my moneyboxes," said Julian, guiltily.

"Oh, Julian!" Pat groaned.

The next day, everything was ready for the Jumble Sale.

Julian and Meera arrived with their moneybox pigs.

"Look, Dad!" said Julian proudly.

"My word, Julian. They're just grand," smiled Pat.

"Thank you, children," said Nisha. "We'll put them next to Ajay's old toolboxes."

"I tell you what, Nisha," said Sara. "Those toolboxes are just what I need!"

Pat went to chat to Bill and Alf.

"Dorothy not here, then?" he asked.

"No, Mum couldn't come," said Bill. "She's got a sore throat from shouting at the crows!"

"Poor Dorothy!" Pat exclaimed. "But I've got an idea – there's something I need to buy."

The vicar had his eye on something too. He patted his violin case fondly.

"Nisha, would you think it most selfish of me to buy back my old violin?"

"Of course not, Reverend!" Nisha replied.

"What the Lord has joined together, let no one put asunder!" beamed the vicar.

Meanwhile, Pat had had another recycling brainwave!

"You see, Dr Gilbertson, you just fold the sewing machine over, like this, and the whole thing turns into a table."

"Perfect," Dr Gilbertson giggled. "You're a genius, Pat!"

The Jumble Sale was a great success. Pat stopped at the Thompson's farm on his way home.

"Hello, Dorothy. I've got a surprise for you." Pat put the cuckoo clock on the lettuce patch.

"Cuck-oooo! Cuck-ooooo!" it warbled.

"Aark! Aark!" The crows flew off in alarm.

"Pat, you're a marvel!" laughed Dorothy.

When Pat got home, Sara had planted her geraniums – in Ajay's toolboxes.

"What a clever idea," said Pat. "You made toolboxes into window boxes!"

"Well, it is Recycling Week," Sara smiled.

"And we sold all our moneyboxes," said Meera.

"Except for one," added Julian. "This is for you, Dad. After all, I did use your newspaper!"

"Thank you," grinned Pat. "It's amazing what you can do with other people's rubbish!"

SIMON AND SCHUSTER
First published in 2006 in Great Britain by Simon & Schuster UK Ltd
Africa House, 64-78 Kingsway
London WC2B 6AH

Postman Pat® © 2006 Woodland Animations, a division of Entertainment Rights PLC
Licensed by Entertainment Rights PLC
Original writer John Cunliffe
From the original television design by Ivor Wood
Royal Mail and Post Office imagery is used by kind permission of Royal Mail Group plc
All rights reserved

Text by Alison Ritchie © 2006 Simon & Schuster UK Ltd

A CIP catalogue record for this book is available from the British Library upon request

ISBN 1416910549

Printed in China

1 3 5 7 9 10 8 6 4 2